ONLY FOR A WHILE

AuthorHouse™ LLC
1663 Liberty Drive
Bloomington, IN 47403
www.authorhouse.com
Phone: 1-800-839-8640

Published by AuthorHouse 03/21/2014

ISBN: 978-1-4918-7432-5 (sc)
ISBN: 978-1-4918-7433-2 (e)

Library of Congress Control Number: 2014905215

This book is printed on acid-free paper.

ONLY FOR A WHILE

The Journey of Rosebud Bear

Connie Mygatt

authorHOUSE®

Prologue

The late spring rising sun sent a beam of light through the front display window of NELLIE'S ANTIQUES AND USABLE JUNK SHOP. For a few minutes the sun rested upon an open dust-covered wooden box filled with old discarded toys. The box had been sitting in the same spot on the floor for a long time. The head of a stuffed giraffe drooped over the side of the box. Close to the giraffe were dolls in various shapes and sizes with dirty, dusty faces and matted hair. And, in one corner of the box, barely visible, rested an old stuffed bear.

The bear's stuffing had become lumpy and much of it had escaped through tears and holes in the body. Her covering was stained and dirty; all of the printed pink rosebuds on her cloth body were faded or completely gone. Even some of her repair patches were frayed away to thin threads. Her once bright red satin heart had frayed to a heart-shaped fringe.

The warm sun slowly reached part of the bear's face. It rested there for a brief moment, stirring a deep sigh from within her. She opened her eyes and tried to move, but it was pointless. The toys surrounding her rested heavily on her frail body, preventing her from moving.

As the sun continued on its journey, the bear sighed and drifted off to sleep for the thousandth time. Her thoughts began to mingle with her dreams and she was once again in the gentle hands of Mrs. Tucker, being created, stitch by stitch into a soft, cuddly bear for her daughter Hannah's birthday. That was years . . . and . . . years ago.

Chapter 1

"Happy Birthday, Hannah! Close your eyes and hold out your arms because I have a wonderful birthday surprise for you," Hannah's mother said. Hannah grinned and tightly squeezed her eyes shut. As the gift was placed in Hannah's arms she quickly opened her eyes and saw a smiling sweet bear, with small pink rosebuds on a white cotton background all over her body. She touched the smooth red satin heart and cradled the bear in her arms, which were a perfect fit for the bear.

"Oh, Mama, I just love this bear," Hannah said as she cuddled her special gift close to her heart. The bear felt her first emotion. Love. A feeling that warmed her to the very center of her soft stuffing.

"Wherever did you get that beautiful fabric?" Gran Ann asked Hannah's mother.

"I found it in Lindy's Fabric store. It reminded me of the flour sack fabrics that you used to sew into dresses for me when I was Hannah's age. I knew it was special the minute I saw it and decided it would make a wonderful bear for Hannah's seventh birthday. The blue pearl eyes are buttons from a dress you made for me when I was a little girl. I knew this was the right place to use them because they match Hannah's beautiful blue eyes."

"Oh, Mama, you sewed my name on the bear's foot. It says 'Hannah's Bear'." Hannah gently moved her fingers over the tiny stitches.

Hugging her daughter, Mrs. Tucker said, "That's right, Hannah, a special bear for my special girl."

"What are you going to name the bear, Hannah?" Gran Ann asked.

"That's easy. I'll call her 'Rosebud' because she has so many beautiful pink rosebuds all over her. Oh, beautiful Rosebud, I love you." Hannah squeezed Rosebud so tightly that her stuffing almost squeaked. Rosebud felt her first giggle, which made her stuffing feel like it was dancing. She looked at Hannah's big blue eyes, long curly hair, and happy smile. "I love you, too," she said silently from her heart.

Hannah and Rosebud became best friends. They snuggled together every night, played together during the day, read books, and colored and painted together. Rosebud loved their parties with Hannah's friends.

On special days she went to school with Hannah. All the children loved her, even the boys. They all wanted their mothers to make them bears. But no one could make a bear quite like Rosebud.

When Hannah was thirteen years old, Rosebud began to realize things were beginning to change. She knew Hannah still loved her, but it seemed that her friend kept getting bigger and bigger and they were spending less time together.

"Maybe if I stretch out my arms and legs I'll get bigger too." But no matter how hard Rosebud stretched, she remained the same size. And it made her sad.

Hannah could always tell when her little bear was unhappy. Her stuffing seemed to sink in on itself making her look very small. "Don't you ever be sad, my dear little bear. You will always be my best friend."

"Little bear," Rosebud repeated to herself. "If I just remember Hannah loves me, it doesn't matter what size I am."

Chapter 2

One day, not long after Hannah turned sixteen, she came home from school very excited. "Mama, Gran Ann, guess what?" Hannah shouted as she flung open the front door. Rosebud was sitting on Gran Ann's rocker. Gran Ann and Mama quickly came to the hallway from the kitchen.

"What is all the excitement, Hannah?" they both asked.

"Remember, I told you that when I turned sixteen I could try out for the cheerleading team?" Mrs. Tucker nodded. A proud grin filled Hannah's face. "Well, I tried out and I made the team. I'm now a cheerleader!"

"But that's not the best part," she quickly added. "We all voted to have Rosebud as our mascot, for good luck. I told them you would make her a little cheerleader outfit."

"What a wonderful idea, Hannah. I'd be happy to do that."

At first Rosebud didn't like the idea of being turned into a mascot. She rather liked being a bear. She soon found out that she was still totally herself with the addition of her own cheerleading outfit. At football games and pep rallies, she was tossed in the air, hugged, cried on and spilled upon and always loved by everyone.

Chapter 3

The next two years flew by quickly. Rosebud noticed that she was spending more and more time on Hannah's bed waiting for her to return. Hannah's life was busy with parties, dances, meetings, graduation from high school, and a part-time summer job at the Frosty Freeze.

Rosebud knew she couldn't go everywhere with Hannah. She had become used to that when Hannah stopped putting her in her backpack. The books had gotten bigger and there were so many more books that there simply wasn't any room for her. She contented herself with the fact that at the end of the day Hannah would always come home and cuddle with her at night. Before falling asleep Hannah always shared the many exciting things that had happened during the day.

Toward the end of the summer around the time that Hannah turned eighteen, Rosebud watched her pack some of her clothing in a trunk and some of her books and pictures into a box.

Hannah sat on the edge of the bed and for a few minutes didn't say or do anything. Finally she reached over and took Rosebud in her arms and said, "I'm going away for a while. To a place called college where I will learn to be a teacher. There will be so many new experiences for me. To tell you the truth, I'm a little scared."

Rosebud didn't know what scared was but she didn't think it was a good way to feel.

"I can't take you with me. I'm going to have two other girls in my room, and it is a small room. I just don't know if it would be a safe place for you. I promise if everything goes well maybe I can take you back with me after the Christmas vacation."

Rosebud felt her stuffing get tight. She didn't really understand what she was being told, but Hannah looked sad and that made her sad too.

"I'll really miss you, but I know you will be safe here at home. And, as I said, it will only be for a while."

Rosebud had no idea what or where college was, and she wondered how long *a while* was. Sadness gripped her heart as she watched Hannah leave the room. As a tiny tear dropped from one blue pearl eye, Rosebud wanted to cry, "Please, take me with you!"

Chapter 4

Days and weeks passed. Rosebud began to realize that *a while* seemed like a very long time. Just when she thought she couldn't spend one more day alone, Rosebud saw Mrs. Tucker walk into Hannah's room. A little girl with two long red braids of hair hanging over her shoulders followed behind her.

"Rebecca, this is Hannah's room. While your Aunt Mary and I visit, you can play with the special toys Hannah saved," Mrs. Tucker said as she lifted the lid of the wooden chest.

Rebecca stood staring and smiling at the stuffed bear on the bed. "May I please play with this beautiful bear, Mrs. Tucker?"

"Why of course you may, Rebecca. Her name is Rosebud. I made her for Hannah when she was your age. She was always

Hannah's best friend." Mrs. Tucker patted Rebecca on the head and left the room.

As Rebecca picked up Rosebud one red braid fell forward and tickled Rosebud's nose. "Hello Rosebud. What a wonderful name you have. My name is Rebecca."

Rosebud giggled. Looking at the girl's face, she thought, "Wow! Rebecca, you have freckles all over your face just like I have rosebuds on mine. I guess we have something in common."

Rebecca took Hannah's tea set from a shelf and placed it on the floor. "Let's have a tea party, Rosebud."

Rebecca spent the afternoon talking. She told the bear funny stories and sad stories and happy stories. Rosebud felt like her whole body was a big smile and that her seams were about to burst with delight to have a new friend.

When it was time for Rebecca to go, she didn't want to part with Rosebud.

"Mrs. Tucker, may I please, please take her to my Aunt Mary's house," she asked while looking lovingly at the little bear in her arms. "I promise I will take very good care of her. Oh, please, may I?"

At first Mrs. Tucker wasn't sure it was a good idea. She rubbed her hand over her chin and thought for a minute.

"You two look so happy together. And I know you will take good care of her for Hannah. I guess it will be all right for a while, Rebecca," Mrs. Tucker said.

"Oh, dear," thought Rosebud, "there's the words *a while* again. I don't know if I want to go away for *a while*."

Hugging Mrs. Tucker, Rebecca exclaimed, "Thank you, Mrs. Tucker! We will sure have fun together."

Rosebud was very excited. She also felt something else and remembered another word that Hannah said, "scared." Yes, excited and scared. Just the way Hannah felt when she left for college. Rosebud had never left the house except with Hannah. "Golly," she thought, "I hope Hannah doesn't come home while I'm gone.

Chapter 5

For two weeks Rebecca and her new friend had a wonderful time together. They went shopping with Aunt Mary. They had picnics in the park. The most fun they had was a trip to the zoo to see big black furry bears, white polar bears, and panda bears. "They aren't as lucky as I am," thought Rosebud. "They don't have one single rosebud on them."

Rosebud heard Aunt Mary tell Rebecca that bears hibernate, which meant they go to sleep in a dark place during the winter. "Ah," thought Rosebud, "that's what I do a lot. I hibernate."

When it came time for Rebecca to go home, Rosebud didn't feel too sad. She liked Rebecca very much, but she was tired and wanted to take a long nap on Hannah's bed.

Unfortunately, Rebecca had other plans. "I have a secret to tell you. I'm not going to send you back to Mrs. Tucker's house. There is just something so special about you and I need to take you home with me for a while longer."

All Rosebud heard were two words, *a while.* Once more her stuffing tightened. She worried whether Hannah would ever find her.

Rosebud felt her soft body being placed into the middle of freshly washed jeans, shirts, dresses, socks, shoes, pajamas, and underwear. She could hardly breathe. "Hannah always carried me in her arms when we went away," she cried. Rosebud did not like being hidden in a suitcase at all!

Chapter 6

Rebecca arrived home to big hugs and many kisses from her parents. "It is so good to have you home. We missed you," they said.

"I missed you too!" Rebecca said, hugging her parents back. "Aunt Mary said I'm big enough to unpack my own suitcase. Can I do it to show you what a big girl I am?"

"That would be wonderful, Rebecca," her mother said as she carried the suitcase to Rebecca's room and placed it on the bed.

"I have freshly baked oatmeal and raisin cookies in the kitchen. Come down when you're finished, dear." When Rebecca's mother left the room, Rebecca quickly opened her suitcase. She tossed jeans, dresses, and shoes until she finally pulled out a squashed Rosebud.

"Rosebud, I'm sorry I had to hide you in my suitcase," Rebecca said as she readjusted some of Rosebud's stuffing. Rosebud took a deep breath to help fluff up her stuffing. She looked around Rebecca's room. It was a nice enough room, but it wasn't Hannah's room. The window was smaller and higher up. She didn't think she would be able to see out of it as she could from Hannah's bed.

Placing Rosebud on her knee, Rebecca leaned close to Rosebud's ear and whispered, "No one must ever find you. Here is my plan. When we're not playing in my room you will have to stay in my closet. When we are playing, we'll play next to my bed so I can push you under it if my mommy should come in."

"Well," thought Rosebud, "I didn't need to worry about not seeing out of the window from the bed. I won't see anything from the closet." It all made Rosebud feel very, very homesick.

Rebecca felt a little nervous about her plan. "Rosebud, I don't feel very good about not telling my parents about you, but since Aunt Mary never mentioned that it was time to return you to Mrs. Tucker's house, I felt no one would really miss you. So, I didn't think it would matter too much if you just happened to end up in my suitcase and go home with me for a while."

Rebecca knew that if she told that story to her mother she would send the bear right back to Mrs. Tucker. She just was not ready to part with her new friend; there was no other way but to keep her secret hidden from her parents.

Rosebud was relieved to be out of the suitcase, but she didn't like the idea of being Rebecca's secret possession or at hearing the words *a while* again. Her blue pearl eyes began to glisten with tears.

Just like everyone else who had ever met Rosebud, Rebecca could sense Rosebud's feelings. "Rosebud, we'll have a lot of fun. I promise you we will."

Chapter 7

Rosebud soon found out that Rebecca was right. They did have fun when they played together. Regardless, it was still no fun being hidden in the closet.

One day Rebecca put Rosebud in her backpack and took her to her friend Elizabeth's house. Through a little hole  in the backpack Rosebud could see Elizabeth's face. She had more freckles than Rebecca. Rosebud felt happy about that, but the best thing about Elizabeth was her little tree house.

As Rebecca climbed the ladder to the tree house, Rosebud watched the ground get farther and farther away. "This is a little scary," thought Rosebud. She could feel her stuffing turn and tighten with each step up the ladder.

With a soft giggle, Rebecca gently lifted Rosebud from her backpack and introduced her to Elizabeth who of course instantly fell in love with the rosebud-covered bear.

Rosebud looked around the tiny room. She saw lots of toys and books and a small table and chairs. Through the window she could see tiny birds chirping happily on the sprawling branches of an oak tree.

Elizabeth placed a delicious lunch of peanut butter and jelly sandwiches, red grapes, cookies, and small cans of apple juice on the table. Both Rebecca and Elizabeth pretended to share their lunch with Rosebud. The smell of peanut butter made Rosebud homesick for Hannah. Peanut butter and strawberry jelly was Hannah's favorite sandwich.

Over lunch, after latching little fingers and doing a pinky swear to keep her secret, Rebecca shared with Elizabeth the true story about how this cute bear happened to be in her life.

The three of them played in the tree house all afternoon until, from the base of the tree, Elizabeth's mother called out that Rebecca's mother had arrived to take her home.

The three were sad to see the day end. Elizabeth came up with a quick plan of her own and shared it with Rebecca. "Rebecca, Rosebud really likes my tree house. I think this is a much better place for her to hide. I think I should keep her here."

Rebecca quickly put Rosebud in her backpack telling Elizabeth, "Rosebud doesn't like to be away from me at all. So you see, even if I wanted to leave her here, she wouldn't want to stay." Stuffed in the backpack, Rosebud thought, "Golly, I'd much rather stay in Elizabeth's wonderful tree house than in the closet."

As if Rebecca heard Rosebud's thoughts, she said, "Elizabeth, I promise I'll bring Rosebud with me every time I come over to play." Elizabeth and Rosebud both liked that idea.

That night, as Rosebud tried to fall asleep in the dark closet, she felt a great pang of sadness. She had really enjoyed the day, but all the fun she had could not replace her longing for Hannah.

Weeks went by and Rebecca's secret plan was going perfectly well until one afternoon when Rebecca and Rosebud were reading on the bed. Rebecca began to yawn and before long they were both sound asleep.

"Rebecca, honey, wake up. It's time for dinner," Rebecca's mother said.

Lifting Rosebud from the bed, her mother asked, "Where did you get this cute bear?" Rebecca pretended to be asleep. She didn't want to tell her mother the truth about Rosebud.

"Come on, Rebecca, wake up. Does the bear belong to Elizabeth?"

"Huh?" Rebecca yawned while squeezing her eyes to keep them shut. She considered saying that Rosebud belonged to Elizabeth. But quickly decided that was not a good idea because her mother would give the bear to Elizabeth. Plus, Elizabeth's mother would tell her the bear didn't belong to Elizabeth. She realized she had to tell the truth.

Slowly, Rebecca opened her eyes. She saw her mother holding Rosebud. "She's not just a bear, Mommy. She's special. Her name is Rosebud!"

"Where did Rosebud come from, Rebecca?"

Rosebud felt sorry for Rebecca. She hoped she wouldn't be in too much trouble. Heaving out a big sigh, Rebecca swung her legs over the side of the bed and looked at the floor. "She came from Aunt Mary's." Rebecca started chewing on the end of one of her braids, a sure sign to her mother that her answer wasn't the complete truth.

"Did Aunt Mary give her to you?"

"Well . . . not really," Rebecca said, still chewing her braid and looking at the floor. Her mother sat next to her on the bed. "Rebecca, do you have something you want to tell me?"

"No! I mean, Yeah . . . I guess . . . I do. I . . . sort of . . . borrowed her for a while. A friend of Aunt Mary's said I could borrow her."

"Did Aunt Mary's friend say you could bring the bear home?" Rebecca didn't answer, but just kept looking at the floor.

"I take it that means no. Rebecca, if you borrow something, that doesn't mean it's yours to keep. Rosebud must go back to Aunt Mary's friend tomorrow. I'll call Aunt Mary for the address. After dinner I want you to write a letter and apologize for keeping Rosebud."

Rosebud liked Rebecca's mommy. She had a gentle voice like Mrs. Tucker's. Rosebud also liked the thought that she would no longer need to be in the closet. She was no longer a secret. And, "Best of all," she thought, "tomorrow I go home to Hannah!"

A tearful Rebecca hugged her little friend all night long. Rosebud was sad that Rebecca had gotten into trouble. But, as she drifted off to sleep, she couldn't help but think that soon she would be back in Hannah's arm sleeping in her warm, cozy bed.

The next morning a very sad Rebecca held Rosebud close to her heart while her mother called Aunt Mary to get Mrs. Tucker's address. Rosebud really liked Rebecca and Elizabeth too, but the both of them didn't equal one Hannah in her heart. What she did hope was that someone would make Rebecca her very own bear to love because she really had a lot of love to give.

Chapter 8

The next morning Rosebud listened to Rebecca's tearful sobs as she was carefully placed in a cardboard box to be mailed back to Mrs. Tucker.

Days passed slowly. There were times when Rosebud heard the hum of a motor, much louder than the one in the Tuckers' family car. She hoped she was getting closer to home. Finally, her cardboard box came to rest on a flat surface. Time wasn't a concept that Rosebud understood, but she did think that this was a long *a while*, much longer than other *a whiles*.

She drifted in and out of sleep.

Then, one day someone picked up the box she was in and she heard a voice say, "Joe, were you able to make out any of the address on this smeared label?"

"I don't think so, Fred," Joe replied. "All I can make out is a Mr. or could be Mrs. T. Looks like something was spilled on the box and if there was a return label, it is gone."

From inside the box Rosebud finally realized why she felt so damp.

"Just open it up and see if there is any information on the inside," she heard the gruff-voiced Fred say.

As Joe opened the box, a flood of bright light startled Rosebud. She squinted several times before being fully able to focus. She smiled with gratitude as she watched a young man with a large grin and a very big mustache lift her from the box.

"No address, Fred. But, there is a note and a very cute but musty little bear."

Fred took the note while Joe stood holding Rosebud. She watched as the much older man read the note.

"Dear Rosebud's Mommy," Fred read the large printed words out loud. "I'm very sorry I took Rosebud home for a visit. I really love her a lot. Sincerely, Rebecca."

"Well, there's no information here. We'll just put the note and the bear back in the box and hope someone sends out a search for a lost box with a stuffed bear inside. Pack it all back up and send it over to regional's dead letter department," Fred said, handing the note to Joe.

As Joe placed Rosebud back in the box and crisscrossed and folded the flaps in securely, she heard him say, "I sure hope someone claims you, little bear. You are just too cute to sit on a shelf." Rosebud sure hoped so too.

The box sat on a shelf with other forgotten and lost mail in the lost letter department. Rosebud didn't know how long she had been there, but did know it was a long hibernation. Long enough to gather a lot of dust through small openings in the flaps, which made her sneeze.

Rosebud spent most of her days just sleeping and dreaming about Hannah. Since the day she arrived at her present place, no one had reached for her box. She pretty much thought she would never be found and began to go back to sleep when she heard a very loud a . . . choo as she felt the box being lifted from the shelf.

Dust fell on Rosebud's body as someone pulled open the flaps of the box. She felt a woman's strong but gentle hand lift her up and begin to brush the dust from her face.

"What do we have here?" Rosebud looked into the smiling face of a woman who looked a lot like Gran Ann except she didn't have gray hair. After being in the box in one position for so long, her stuffing felt hard and lumpy. She felt her insides come to life by the warmth of the woman's hands.

"Well, I do declare. I bet you were a cutie at one time. Maybe a warm bath would clean ya up. I sure didn't know I would find a treasure like you when I was asked to clean up the shelves in here. They said to just throw the things away, but you, little bear, I think I will take home."

She put Rosebud aside and continued with her work. When it came time to go home, she picked up Rosebud and said, "I'm Shirley. Even with the moldy spots and dust, there is something rather special about you, little bear. I bet one of the kids in the neighborhood would like to have you."

As Shirley, her new friend, carried her home in a string carry-all bag, one thought started Rosebud's heart beating again, "Maybe I'll soon see Hannah."

When Shirley got home, she filled the kitchen sink with warm, sudsy water. Lifting her precious find from the string bag, she tenderly placed her in the water and gently washed

the dust and mold from her
face and body. After rinsing
off all the soap, she placed
Rosebud in a soft white
towel and sat her on a chair
near the heater to dry.

Rosebud felt pure
contentment from Shirley's loving care. She sat looking out
the window at a dark star-filled sky. It wasn't long before she
fell into a deep, peaceful, happy sleep.

The next morning Shirley picked up the dry bear and
looked her over. She looked at the foot and saw some of the
letters were beginning to fray. The first letter was almost
gone, a few stitches from some of the other letters were
missing, and the last letter of the second word was frayed
beyond recognition. Rosebud wished she could tell her it said
"Hannah's Bear," that is who she belonged to, Hannah.

"You were well loved by someone," Shirley said, placing
her back on the chair. "Next time I see my neighbor's little
girl, Susie, I'll give you to her. I know she will love you."

In less than a week, Shirley placed a big pink bow around Rosebud's neck and presented her to Susie. Susie was delighted and gave Shirley a big hug. What Shirley told Rosebud was true. It was love at first sight for Susie. She adored her soft cuddly present. She decided to name her after herself and called her Susie Bear, Susie B for short. Rosebud did not like her new name, but she did like Susie and decided that while she was waiting for Hannah to find her she would put up with being called Susie B.

What Shirley didn't know was that Susie's older brother, Joey, had turned into a tease that bordered on a bully. He didn't like girly things and felt that Susie was just a tattle-tale who was always getting him in trouble. Trouble that he deserved, but nonetheless, he was always looking for a way to get even.

For a while Rosebud just rested on Susie's bed while she went off to school or piano lessons. Then one day Joey, who was mad at his sister again, picked up Rosebud and decided to use her for a game of catch with his buddies.

"Joseph Martin. Give me back my bear!" Susie cried as she watched Rosebud being tossed through the sprinkler, turned, pulled, and dropped until her little body was covered with dirt and one arm began to tear. Rosebud was really scared. No one had ever treated her like that before.

Susie stomped toward the house yelling, "I'm telling Mom on you!"

Joey tossed the bear at Susie. "Here's your dumb bear, cry baby." Joey hadn't finished his sentence before their mother opened the kitchen screen door and let it slam loudly behind her. Susie stood holding the bear tightly in one arm while wiping tears that had collected at the bottom of her chin with the other arm. Rosebud's stuffing trembled. Her arm dangled over Susie's arm and she felt dirty and wet to the center of her stuffing.

Susie's mother was very angry. "Joey, that is it! You are grounded for a month!"

Rosebud watched Joey's friends run from the yard. "Don't think you are getting away with this, Matty and Philip," Susie's mother yelled to them. "I'm going to call your mothers."

As she grabbed Joey's arm and marched him toward the house, he whispered to Susie, "You and your stupid bear better watch out."

Not one word missed his mother's ears. "Joey, when are you going to learn, it is you yourself that gets you into trouble. And, by the way, that just added no television for the month."

Susie couldn't help but feel a slight twinge of satisfaction, no, actually a big bunch of satisfaction for all the trouble Joey got into for treating Susie B so badly. She was glad for that, but very sad at what he and his friends had done to her new friend.

Susie took her sad-looking bear to her bathroom where she tried to wash off most of the mud. She used her hair dryer to plump up the stuffing. Rosebud began to relax as the warm air from the dryer filled her body.

"I'm so sorry, Susie B. I'm going to hide you some place where Joey can't find you for a while."

There were those words, *a while*, again and by now Rosebud knew that did not mean anything good.

Susie took Rosebud to the garage. Back in a corner sat an old dresser.

Holding the bear in front of her, she said, "Susie Bear, Joey would never think of looking in here for you. You will be safe and I can take you out to play anytime I want to and put you back here when we aren't playing." Giving the bear a kiss on her nose, she placed her in the back of the bottom drawer, leaving it open just a little so she would get some air. From the opening Rosebud could see a long sliver of light next to her.

"Well," Rosebud thought, "here I am again, hiding. It is good I like to sleep, because I sure do a lot of it." Within minutes Rosebud drifted off to sleep glad she was in a safe place.

Susie felt happy about her secret hiding place for her sweet bear. Happy until she remembered that Joey was grounded for a month. It would be difficult to retrieve and return Susie B from her hiding place. Susie also didn't know that her best friend's mother had invited her to join them on their summer road trip. She would be a birthday surprise for her best friend.

During dinner, Susie found out about the trip that started the next day. Of course, with all the excitement, she had forgotten about Susie B. She didn't remember until the next afternoon when she saw cute stuffed animals lining a shelf in a gift shop next to the restaurant where they stopped for lunch. The size of the lump in her throat kept her from enjoying her lunch. She worried about her bear, but finally decided that Susie B would be perfectly safe in the drawer during her absence.

Upon returning, Susie ran to the garage to get Susie B and tell her all about her adventures. When she saw that a new workbench stood in the place where the bear's hiding place had been, she let out a howl that brought her mother, father, and Joey running from the house.

"Susie, what is the matter? Are you hurt?" her mother asked.

"No, Susie . . . . B . . . . is gone!" Susie cried between sobs. "I put her in the dresser drawer to keep her from Joey and she is gone."

"Susie, I am sorry. We had no idea the bear was in the drawer. It was empty when we put it in the garage. We never thought to look inside again," her father said, looking very sad as he took Susie in his arms.

Susie could not be comforted, and when her father said he would buy her a new bear, Susie's sobs just got louder.

"Who bought the dresser? Maybe we can call him and get Susie B back," Susie's mother said to her father.

"He didn't give me his name. He said he was heading home and saw the dresser by the driveway and wanted to purchase it. He paid cash. I think he said his name was Vincent, but he never gave me his last name."

Of course that news just made Susie cry harder.

That night, in bed, Susie thought about Susie B. No other bear could ever replace her, of that she was sure. She just hoped whoever bought the chest didn't have a brother like Joey.

Chapter 9

It was Vincent Angelo who, a week earlier, bought the dresser from Susie's father. When he opened the drawers to check how easily they opened and closed, he never noticed Rosebud in the bottom drawer.

He purchased the dresser for his wife, Maria, who was a seamstress and dressmaker. When he arrived home, she was sitting on the porch. "Maria, come see what I bought for you for your shop."

From the partially opened drawer, Rosebud could see a rosy-cheeked lady with short gray hair. A neighbor came over and helped Vincent lift the chest from the truck. They placed it in the garage where Mr. Angelo could clean it up and give it a fresh coat of paint.

Maria began opening and closing the drawers. "Oh my, Vincent, this will be a wonderful place to store my very special fabrics."

When she opened the bottom drawer and saw Rosebud, she chuckled. "Vincent, did you pay extra for this little guy?"

Rosebud thought, "Guy, indeed. I'm a girl!"

Maria turned Rosebud around and looked her over. "Someone made this little bear, Vincent. It was very well made at one time. Oh look, a name is stitched on the foot. Many of the letters are missing. I think it might have said 'Anna's Bea,' probably bear. Well, I will call her Anna. A few patches, and sewing the arm on tightly will help her look much better. She will be wonderful to have in the shop for the children to play with." Tucking Rosebud under her arm, Maria headed toward the kitchen. When Rosebud heard Maria turn on the kitchen faucet, she was very glad that she would be getting a bath.

Several days later Rosebud discovered that Maria was a very fine seamstress. She was washed, restuffed, stitched, and patched with tiny swatches of fabric that also had very tiny pink rosebuds on them. She sat proudly upon a soft cushion on a rocking chair in Maria's shop.

From the rocker she looked around her new surroundings and saw a small fire-stove in one corner of the shop. Near it was a table with an electric kettle for Maria to serve her patrons tea. Under a large window, overlooking the street, sat a purple sofa with colorful pillows in the corners. Next to the sofa were some games and children's books. Rosebud liked this room. She thought it a good place to be until Hannah found her.

Maria made beautiful clothing for women and children. Not a day went by without people coming into Maria's shop. Rosebud, now answering to the name Anna, was filled with joy that someone loved her and didn't need to hide her away! The children who arrived with the adults always played with her. Maria never allowed Rosebud to be mistreated, and if part of her fabric began to get thin from all the hugs and attention, Maria added a brand-new patch.

Sometimes the little girls reminded Rosebud of Hannah. Maybe a smile or giggle or blue eyes and curly brown hair or just the way someone held her brought warm memories that made her both happy and sad.

One day, after an active morning of play, Rosebud was on the floor under the table where Maria sat and talked to customers. She heard the bell on the front door jingle and two women walked in. Maria greeted them by the door. She saw Maria nod when she was handed a photograph. A chair was in the way of seeing the two women. All Rosebud could see were skirts and shoes as they approached the table and sat down.

Rosebud felt a gentle nudge from a woman's shoe as it brushed past her body. She felt an excitement that she didn't understand. There was something about the two ladies that made her want to cry with joy when she heard their voices.

"Your daughter will look beautiful in this dress," Maria said. "But, unfortunately, I will not be able to make it for her. I have three other wedding dresses to make. I can give you the name of a friend who might have the time and is a very good seamstress."

"Mrs. Angelo, I'm so sorry you can't make my dress for me. You made my best friend's dress and it was beautiful. I was just hoping . . ." Rosebud's heart began to beat rapidly as she heard the young woman speak.

The other woman finished the sentence for her. "Hannah was hoping there would be enough time for you to make her dress."

Rosebud did not hear the end of the sentence. All she heard was the name "Hannah" said by a woman whose voice she had known since her first stitches. Hannah and her mother were almost in touching distance! Her heart continued to beat so fast she thought it would burst.

Rosebud heard the chairs being pushed back under the table and watched the two women walk toward the door. Between the two chairs all she could see was Hannah's hand reaching for the door knob.

"No! No, don't go, Hannah. I'm here under the table!" At that moment she wished with all her heart that she had a real voice. She watched Hannah walk out the door as her heart broke in several places that she felt could never be repaired.

During the next few weeks, every time the door bell jingled Rosebud made a wish that it would be Hannah again, but as weeks turned into months, she finally gave up hope. "Well," she thought, "at least I did get to see her hand and hear her voice. That was wonderful. And I know she isn't far away. She will find me!"

Chapter 10

Another year went by and Rosebud once again settled into the life of being the best-loved bear that ever was. Boys and girls wanted to take her home, but Maria would never part with her. Rosebud was just too special, which, of course, made Rosebud feel very happy.

Then one night Rosebud heard the sound of a siren get louder and louder and stop outside the Angelos' house. From the rocker in the shop, Rosebud could see out the shop window. Her stuffing tightened when she saw Maria being carried on a stretcher to an ambulance. Mr. Angelo was right behind the stretcher. Once more the sirens began to blare in the night's stillness and she longed to go with Maria. She sat in her rocking chair watching as night turned into day.

Ruby, a seamstress who worked for Maria, came to the shop the next morning and hung a sign on the front door. Rosebud could see the sign as Ruby walked toward the door. It said CLOSED UNTIL FURTHER NOTICE. Ruby stopped and sadly looked around the shop, then walked to the telephone on the table. Rosebud heard her make several phone calls. Tears were falling down Ruby's face as she walked past the rocker. Rosebud's heart sank as she watched Ruby open the door and heard her lock it behind her. She didn't understand what was going on, only that Maria was gone and that made her feel scared and sad.

A few days later the house and shop were filled with people, mostly wearing black. Rosebud could hear people talking

about how kind, creative, and smart Maria had been.

Rosebud listened to people laugh as they told endearing and funny stories about Maria. "I wish I could tell my stories about Maria. I would tell about how she made me giggle when she gave me a bath in lots of bubbles. Or about how she always patted me on the head and said 'love you, little Anna' before she went through the shop door to the house at the end of day." She liked just thinking about all the happy times with Maria.

During the following weeks, Mr. Angelo sat many nights in Maria's shop on the sofa looking at photo albums. Rosebud watched tears quietly roll down his face. She was filled with deep sadness too. She wished he would pick her up and hold her in his lap like Maria sometimes did, but Mr. Angelo was not a bear-hugging man. Rosebud knew that, so she just sat in her rocker keeping Mr. Angelo company in his sadness.

Chapter 11

For more than six months Mr. Angelo did not move a thing in Maria's sewing shop. So Rosebud was surprised when she saw two women she had never seen before start to pack up all of Maria's things in boxes. Rosebud felt her body being lifted up and thrown in a box filled with fabric remnants. She liked being in with Maria's fabrics, but she didn't like being put in another box. All the boxes were placed in the back of a pickup truck and driven many miles away.

It was very cold and windy in the back of the pickup. Rosebud felt very sad, lonely, and frightened.

Finally, the truck came to a stop. The flap on Rosebud's box had come open. She heard one woman say to the other, "Let's just leave the things in the truck overnight. I'm too tired to carry anything into the shop tonight." The other woman replied, "Suits me fine."

From the edge of the box Rosebud watched the women walk up a path to a small house. The truck was parked in front of a store with steps leading up to a long covered porch. On the door she read the words, NELLIE'S ANTIQUES AND USABLE JUNK SHOP. As she sank back into Maria's fabric, she said to herself, "Guess I'll be staying here for *a while* too." I wonder if it is closer to where Hannah lives?" were her last thoughts before going back to sleep.

The next morning, Nellie picked up Rosebud from the box of fabrics. "Cute little bear, but lots of patches, probably won't bring much money," she said as she tossed the bear onto a table.

Marcy looked over at the bear. "Yeah, you're probably right. But I bet it made someone happy long ago. Anyway, your mutt, Rags, will find it and have fun with it."

"Ha, that's for sure," Nellie replied, picking up Rosebud, and with the same breath called out to Rags. Rags, a large shaggy-haired mutt of unknown mixed breeds, began wagging his tail when he saw the stuffed bear Nellie held in her hand.

He sniffed Rosebud's face and stood staring at her. The sniffing tickled, but she didn't know what to make of Rags. Rags gently gripped Rosebud between his teeth and took her to his big plump bed. Giving her another sniff, he nudged her over a few inches in the bed and sat looking at her.

Nellie and Marcy laughed. "What's wrong, Rags? It's your bear, you can play with it." Rosebud could feel wet spots from where Rags carried her in his mouth. "Yuck," she thought, "I've seen dogs, but I'm not too happy about being given to one."

From that day on, Rosebud was simply called Bear. Sometimes, Rags gently carried Bear by an arm, a leg, or even the head. But she never felt pain, just wet, either from kisses or saliva.

If Nellie played ball with Rags, Bear watched from the porch. When Rags ate his food, Bear was next to the dish. During endless naps she was by Rags' side. Bear certainly felt loved, but she missed the one-way conversations and the secrets that children shared with her.

At night Rags carried Bear from the shop to the house where he shared a bigger bed with her. When she became

extra dirty, Nellie gave her a bath. Bear thought, "Life is sure different, but good."

Even with her many changing names, her many patches, one new blue button eye, and most of her original pink rosebuds faded away, she never stopped being Hannah's bear, Rosebud.

As the years passed, Rags began spending more and more time in his bed next to Rosebud. The kisses became fewer and fewer.

"Rags, you're not looking so good," Rosebud heard Nellie say one afternoon. Attaching a leash to his collar, she said, "Come on, old boy, it's off to the vet for you."

A day later Bear heard the phone ring. She watched as Nellie slowly put down the phone and say, "Marcy, Rags didn't make it." Bear thought, "Make what? What didn't Rags make?"

A short while later Nellie picked up Bear and placed her on a small table. Bear watched Nellie carry Rags' bed out the front door. She missed her warm, furry buddy. She wondered why Nellie didn't take her with the bed so that they could all be together. Rosebud didn't understand. A part of her knew that Rags would not be coming back.

The next day Nellie gave Bear a bath and placed her in a wooden box with some other toys. Nellie didn't have the heart to throw her away.

Chapter 12

As time passed Rosebud found it very easy to just sleep the days and nights away. Sometimes she exchanged stories with the dolls and Giraffe who shared her little home. They were fascinated by Rosebud's varied and exciting life. After the stories were shared, they took long naps. When they were all awake, they sometimes begged Rosebud to retell one of her stories. When the shop became busy with customers, Giraffe, from the edge of the box, would see an interesting person or event going on and would excitedly share a detailed account of what he saw.

When Marcy retired from the business, Nellie's daughter Julie came to work in the antiques shop. She was young and loved to sing when customers weren't shopping. Rosebud always woke up when Julie sang. Her voice was light and airy and always happy. Giraffe told her friends that Julie was very pretty and that she was always smiling.

One morning Rosebud heard Nellie say to Julie, "I like your ideas about rearranging the shop and giving it a fresh look. At one time I believed that everything I had in the shop would find a new home. I think my idea of recycling will need to be a 'giveaway' for some of these things," Nellie added as she looked around the crowded antiques shop.

Julie replied, "How about we make a big sign that says FREE for some of the things or maybe TWO FREE TREASURES WITH EACH PURCHASE."

There was silence for a few minutes, then Nellie said, "Let's close the place for a few days and just give it a clean sweep."

The next week Nellie, Julie, and a few other women pushed, lifted, dusted, scrubbed, polished furniture, and washed glasses and dishes. The walls were painted eggshell blue. Several pieces of furniture were moved to the covered porch with red tags hanging from pulls or knobs.

Rosebud and her friends felt their little home being lifted up. They stared at a face they didn't know.

"Nellie, what do you want me to do with these old dusty toys?" they heard the woman say.

Nellie looked at the box and said, "That has been sitting there for a long time. No one will buy those old toys. Just throw them in the trash."

As quickly as she said it, she turned. "Oh, wait. I think Bear is in that box. She was my dog's favorite toy."

Nellie reached in the box and lifted out Bear. "Still a cute little bear, but very dusty," she said. Rosebud felt Nellie turn her over and adjust some of her stuffing. "It sure is good to be out of that wooden box," she whispered down to Giraffe. Her stuffing was lumpy and every part of her felt stiff. But she felt a surge of fluffiness as Nellie gently turned and tugged at her body.

Nellie placed Rosebud back in the box and said, "Just take the box to the house. I will wash the bear and maybe the giraffe and see what I can do about the dolls. I can do that for Rags. Maybe I can give them away when they are cleaned up."

Rosebud said to her friends, "This means we could be going to a new home. Someone will surely want each of us."

Giraffe said, "Well, I am sure you are right. I don't know if I will like the bath though."

Rosebud giggled, "Oh, you will like being all cleaned up. It really feels good."

The dolls never had very much to say so they just smiled and thought about how pretty they might look once again.

Chapter 13

A few days later the shop reopened. Many locals stopped to see the shop's new look. Rosebud, Giraffe, and the three dolls did indeed look much better. Nellie had fixed Giraffe's neck so that he once more looked tall and almost elegant. The dolls had new hair and dresses. Each one was placed around the inside of the box so they could be seen. A little sign on the outside said FREE WITH PURCHASE.

The summer months brought many new faces to the shop. Rosebud and her friends watched as old and new shoppers walked past their home on the porch. Sometimes a shopper would pick one of them up and after a brief look, place them back in the box. Giraffe was getting discouraged, which discouraged the dolls too. Rosebud said, "Don't worry. I just know someone will want us." The dolls were reassured. Giraffe remained worried.

Every night the box and other small items on the porch were taken into the shop and brought out during the day. One day the box was placed closer to the entrance.

Rosebud said to her friends, "Now, we can really be seen!"

It was late afternoon and not one person had even glanced at the box. Giraffe and the dolls had fallen asleep. Rosebud drifted in and out of naps. She heard the slam of a car door and heard several footsteps on the porch steps. Two women and a child walked toward the front door. The late afternoon sun shone in Rosebud's eyes so she couldn't make out exactly what they looked like. She started to close her eyes and drift off back to sleep when a tiny hand touched her face and lifted her up from the box. The child giggled as she held Rosebud out in front of her. "You have two different blue eyes and lots of patches, little bear."

Rosebud's heart began to race. "Yes, yes, that is true, but I think I am still cute and would love to go home with you." She felt the little girl turn her around, running her fingers around the once bright pink rosebuds and remaining faded embroidered letters on her foot. Her voice, her giggle flooded Rosebud with thoughts of her Hannah.

Tucking Rosebud under her arm, close to her heart, the girl picked up Giraffe and the dolls one by one and placed them back in the box. From the closed screen door Rosebud heard a voice ask, "Annie, what are you doing out there?"

Rosebud was hanging over Annie's arm and she could not see the lady coming toward them.

"Look, Mommy, this bear has letters on her foot just like your bear did. And she has some rosebuds and lots of patches," she said handing the bear face-first up to her mother.

Rosebud took in a quick breath. Annie's mommy looked like an older Hannah! "Could she be Hannah? Could she be my Hannah?" She felt herself being lifted from Annie's hands. A tender finger traced the worn letters on her foot. "An A, an N, and a B in pink floss," Hannah said in a whisper.

Rosebud felt a tear fall on her face as she heard Hannah say, "Rosebud!"

"Why are you crying, Mommy," Annie asked.

"This is my Rosebud! This bear is Mommy's bear."

Rosebud thought her heart would burst. Hannah finally found her! Just as she always knew she would.

"What have you two found out here?" Rosebud heard an older woman ask.

With great excitement, Hannah and Annie turned to the woman and in unison said, "We found Rosebud!"

"Isn't that exciting, Grandma?" Annie said.

Rosebud watched Mrs. Tucker open the screen door and stop midway when she saw Hannah holding Rosebud.

Extending her arm to Hannah and Rosebud, she said, "Could that really be Rosebud?"

Rosebud felt the now-older hands that gave her life. They traced the remaining threads of stitches where long ago she had attached a red satin heart.

"If home has a feeling, it is right here in my heart," Rosebud thought with a long, deep, peaceful sigh.

Nellie and Julie soon joined them on the porch. "What is all the excitement?"

"How much is this bear? Can you believe I made this for my daughter many years ago when she was about Annie's age?" Mrs. Tucker said.

Nellie clapped her hands and laughed with delight. "Well, she is in the FREE box. I am delighted to say she is yours. Actually, it proves what I have always believed," Nellie added. "There is a place for everything to have a second chance. I knew there was another reason that I just couldn't throw her away."

Hannah took Rosebud from her mother and said, "Come on, Rosebud, it's time to go home."

As they headed toward the car, Annie stopped and turned and asked Nellie, "May I please take her friends with her?"

Nellie picked up the box and handed it to Mrs. Tucker. "I would be delighted to let you have them."

As Mrs. Tucker placed the box in the car, Rosebud heard the dolls giggle for the first time and Giraffe was delighted beyond words.

Annie held Rosebud in front of her and said, "We are taking you home forever and ever." Rosebud was filled with joy. She didn't know what forever and ever was, but she was sure it was longer than *a while.*

The End